I AM
UNDERDOG

D0211797

ANNE SCHRAFF

SADDLEBACK
EDUCATIONAL PUBLISHING

red rhino
b OO k s ™

With more titles on the way …

SADDLEBACK
EDUCATIONAL PUBLISHING
www.sdlback.com

ISBN-13: 978-1-62250-900-3
ISBN-10: 1-62250-900-5
eBook: 978-1-63078-032-6

Printed in Guangzhou, China
NOR/0714/CA21401177

18 17 16 15 14   1 2 3 4 5

KEMBA

Age: 11

Favorite Food: sweet and sour chicken

Favorite Video Game: Underdog

Best Subject in School: math

Best Quality: compassion

UNDERDOG

Age: superheroes live forever

Major Life Event: hurt in a car crash

Goal in Life: helping others

Unique Characteristic: eye patch

Best Quality: bravery

1
NO FRIENDS

"He has no friends." That's what Kemba Spencer's mom said. She spoke in a loud voice. She didn't know Kemba was home.

"I'm worried about him," Dad said. He sounded sad.

Kemba had just gotten home from school. The Pepper Tree School. He was in sixth grade. He stood there. Just listening.

Fingers folding into fists. Hating to hear his parents talk about him like that. Like he was weird. Kemba wanted to punch the wall.

"I don't know." His dad sighed. "What's wrong with him? He's a good kid."

"He's just shy," Mom said.

Kemba was an only child. He wanted his parents to be proud of him. He threw his backpack onto the sofa. Sat down. Punched one of the pillows. Hard. He punched it again. And again. Until his hand hurt.

Knuckles sore

Kemba liked to play computer games. Ones with superheroes. It was fun to pretend he was a hero. Doing exciting things.

Sometimes Kemba dreamed he saved people. From bad guys. From burning buildings. From accidents. Sometimes he won big football games. He would make the winning play. He loved to hear the crowd shouting, "Kem-ba! Kem-ba!"

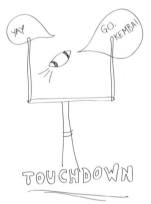

In school nobody cheered for him.

"Look at Kemba."

"He looks like a second grader!"

"You shouldn't be in sixth grade."

"Twerp."

Kemba felt anger wash over him. It made his neck hot. He pounded the pillow again. He listened to his parents' sad voices.

"I had a lot of friends in school," Dad said. Dad was a big man. He had been a big kid. He loved to tell jokes. He loved sports. He was his high school's quarterback. Kemba had seen pictures. "Junior Spencer Won the Game," the headlines read.

"I had lots of friends too," Mom said. "Our house was always full. I had parties. It was fun."

Kemba closed his eyes. He pressed his lips together. Then he grabbed his backpack. Headed for his room.

"Kemba!" Dad looked upset. "How long have you been there?"

"Just got home," Kemba lied.

Dad was afraid Kemba had heard something.

"How was school?" Mom asked.

"Okay," Kemba said.

2
THE BULLY

Kemba hurried to his room. He closed the door. He did his math homework. He liked math. But he did it quickly. He wanted to do what he *really* liked. Play computer games.

MY BIRTHDAY PRESENT FROM AUNT SALLY

Kemba's loved the Underdog series. The

games were about a superhero. He helped the underdogs. The losers. The geeks. The weaker ones. When he saw somebody getting a raw deal? He saved the day. Underdog hated bullies. Kemba hated them too. He hated Richie Mason. He was the biggest bully in school.

RICHIE MASON
~THE MEANEST KID IN THE 6th grade ~

Kemba remembered when he first saw Richie. He was everything Kemba wasn't. He was big. Popular. He looked older. Kids followed him around. He was a huge deal. Nobody laughed at Richie. He looked out for his friends.

But he was a bully.

At lunch Richie yelled, "Follow me, you dudes."

All the boys fell in line. Even Kemba. But Richie turned. "Not you." He smirked. "We don't want you, Spencer."

Kemba got out of line. And he watched. The boys went to a lunch table. It was where they always ate. But today a girl was sitting there. Kemba didn't know her name. She smiled at him once. She seemed nice.

"Hey, you," Richie yelled at her. "Go sit somewhere else. This is our table. It belongs to me. And my friends."

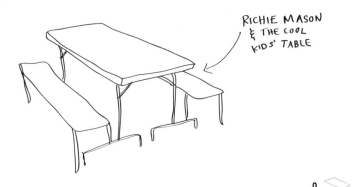

RICHIE MASON & THE COOL KIDS' TABLE

The girl got up. She hurried away.

Kemba usually ignored bullies. But he said, "That was mean."

"Who do you think you're talking to? Punk!" Richie yelled.

Kemba wished he was Underdog. He would fold his arms. He would shout, "I am Underdog. I won't stand for bullies like you!" But he was not Underdog. He was a scared kid.

After lunch Richie and his gang came after him. There were no teachers around. Kemba wanted to run. But he knew they could catch him.

Richie ripped off Kemba's jacket. He threw it into a puddle. It was a new jacket. Kemba liked it a lot. His parents had just bought it. Richie and the other boys laughed. They stomped on it. Then they left, still laughing.

MY JACKET
I ONLY WORE
TWICE

The jacket was cleaned. But Kemba never forgot. It made Kemba sick to remember that day. It made him hate school. He liked his teacher. But he hated everything else. He had no friends. He was small. And shy. Nothing seemed to go right.

Sometimes Kemba even got mad at his hero. Kemba glared at the Underdog poster on his wall. He yelled, "You're a big phony, Underdog!"

3
THE ALLEY

Sometimes Kemba wanted to rip Underdog's poster off the wall. Tear it up. Once, Kemba did try to tear it down. His face was hot with anger. He was shaking. He yanked the poster as hard as he could. But it wouldn't budge. So Kemba sat on the floor. Tears in his eyes. He wasn't really mad at Underdog. He was mad at himself.

In the first game, Kemba learned his hero's story. As a child, Underdog had been hurt. There was a car accident. He lost his left eye. He also had a lot of broken bones. And scars.

Underdog had tan skin. His costume was black and purple. He was a good-looking man. And he wore a cool eye patch.

Kemba was glad he couldn't tear the poster down. Underdog was his friend. His only friend.

At school the next day, Kemba walked

fast. Like always. He didn't look left. Or right. He wanted to get to his class. Sit down. Be safe.

Ms. Clay, his teacher, was nice. She smiled at him. He liked her. But she was not his friend. She was his teacher. He didn't want her to like him too much. It meant trouble. If a teacher liked a kid. Nobody wanted to be teacher's pet. So when she smiled, he'd look down.

Ms. Clay ALWAYS SMILES BIG

He got through the day. Head down. Not drawing attention. That was safest. Don't get seen. Stay low.

After school Kemba took a shortcut home.

He often did that. He liked walking down the alley. It was deserted. Kemba lived three blocks from school. Nobody used the alley. Not like the main street. Kids would tease him there. Yell insults. Make him feel small.

"Hey, shorty! You in first grade?"

"You're weird, Spencer!"

"Aw. Li'l peanut!"

He avoided the main street.

It was getting dark earlier. So he walked faster. He didn't want to be in the alley too late. Halfway through Kemba heard a girl. She screamed.

"No!" she cried. "Let me go!"

Kemba ducked behind a trash can. He was afraid. He turned cold. He hated himself for being chicken. He looked around wildly. If only someone would come. She needed help. Who would do it? Not him.

I'M TOO SKINNY AND A SCAREDY CAT

Kemba saw a boy. He looked about sixteen. He was holding a girl by her arm. She was crying. She looked sixteen too.

"You are mine," the boy shouted. "Don't you forget it!"

Kemba knew him. He was Jabar Mason. Yuck. Richie's big brother. He looked mean, like Richie. Jabar grabbed the girl. He shook her. "Don't you think about leaving me," he screamed. "Ever!"

THE MASONS

RICHIE MASON   JABAR MASON

Kemba's mouth was dry. He couldn't swallow. Couldn't breathe. His heart pounded. *If only somebody would come,* he thought. But nobody did.

4
A SCREAMING VOICE

"Ow," the girl cried. "You're hurting me!"

Kemba was sweating now. It was getting colder. But he was burning up. What could he do? He was a skinny kid. Kemba wished he was Underdog. He would handle this. Underdog was a hero. Kemba was a nobody.

But then Kemba heard it. A voice. High and thin. The voice screeched, "The cops! The cops are here!" The words shook. But they were loud. Fierce.

Jabar let go of the girl. He took off like a rabbit. Like the coward he was. He ran fast. Vanished in seconds.

The girl stood there for a minute. Then she saw Kemba. She came over. "Thanks," she said. "That was really cool." She was shaking. But she managed a smile. "You're my hero."

Then Kemba realized something. *He* had screamed. It was him! He couldn't think of anything else. And it worked. The high, thin warning worked. It had come from *his* mouth. Jabar could scare a girl. But he didn't have the guts to face the cops.

"I'm glad he's gone," Kemba said.

"Yeah," the girl said. "I think he was going to hit me. I used to like him. Just a little bit. We met at a party. He was nice. But then I saw his mean streak. I wanted to break up. He didn't like that."

The girl came closer. "You're just a kid. But you're really brave." She held out her hand. "I'm Rozel Clay."

ROZEL CLAY

Kemba took her hand. "I'm Kemba Spencer."

Rozel's eyes got wide. "Wow! I know your name. My mom is your teacher."

"Ms. Clay is your mom?"

"Yeah, she told me she has this kid. A math whiz. *Kemba*. It's a kinda rare name," Rozel said. She smiled. She was pretty. Like her mom. Kemba was glad he could help her out.

"Bye, Kemba," Rozel said. "And thanks

again. You're cool."

Kemba checked his watch. It was late. He always got home on time. Other kids were late because they were hanging out. Being with friends. Having Fun. But Kemba had zero friends. He had no excuse to be late. Mom would be worried. He had forgotten to charge his phone. It was useless. Buried in his backpack.

He didn't want to worry his parents. But he felt happy inside. He didn't feel that often. But now he did. He helped a girl in trouble. Underdog would do that. It was his thing.

Kemba had never done anything like it. At school Kemba lay low. Even when Richie and his friends were mean. He didn't want trouble. When Richie bumped food trays? He laughed. Spilling kids' lunches was fun. Kemba did nothing. When his own tray was dumped? Kemba did nothing. He just took it.

RICHIE MASON KNOCKED OVER MY MILK

MILK

But today he didn't just take it. He did something brave. He felt warm inside. He felt proud. He felt like he was somebody. Usually his shoulders hunched over. Not now. He walked tall. Straight. Like he was somebody. Maybe what he did wasn't a big deal. Most people would have stopped that creep. But it was a big deal to him. He had done something brave. Heroic.

5
DON'T CALL ME BABY

The door slammed. "Kemba?" Mom called from the kitchen. She came rushing out. "You are so late. I was worried. I tried your phone!"

"Sorry, Mom," Kemba said. "Dead battery."

"You need to keep it charged. That's why you have it! So I don't worry. I wanted to call. See if you were at somebody's house," Mom said. "But I didn't know who to call."

MOM'S FUNNY LOOK

She got a funny look on her face. He knew what she was thinking. She didn't come right out and say it. But she was thinking it. Kemba never spent time at anyone's house. Because he had no friends. It was always that way.

"I was just watching stuff," Kemba said.

Mom looked more worried. "Watching stuff? What stuff? You weren't getting into trouble. Were you, Kemba?"

"No," Kemba said in an angry voice. Then he felt bad. He knew his mom loved him. That was why she worried about him. When somebody loves you, they worry. "I'm sorry, Mom. Some kids were just messing around."

Mom came closer. Her eyes were wide. "You weren't messing with bad kids. Were you?" she asked.

Kemba dumped his backpack on the sofa. He flopped down beside it. "The dudes were skateboarding. It was funny. They kept crashing. I had to laugh. I watched them. That was all," Kemba lied.

"They didn't get mad at you? Did they, Kemba? When you laughed at them," she asked. She was still worried.

Kemba sank deeper into the sofa. He didn't talk to his parents. About being bullied. About bad things. About anything. He never told them about Richie. His pals. What they did. He knew what his parents would do. They would march right to school. They would complain. They would tell the principal that their kid was being bullied.

Kemba knew what would come next. The bullying would get worse. Everybody hated a snitch. Life for Kemba would get even worse.

"Nothing happened, Mom. Everyone was laughing too. They were doing stunts. Ollies. Hippy-jumps. Fakies. They didn't get mad. Okay? It's all good, Mom." Kemba lied again. He was getting good at it. It was easier than telling the truth. Because the truth hurt.

Mom came over. She sat on the sofa beside him. She put her arm around his shoulders. "I just love you so much. My baby. I don't want you to get hurt."

Kemba sighed. He wanted to tell her he

wasn't a baby. But he didn't. His lips moved. No sound came out. He thought, *Please, Mom. It's bad enough. I'm eleven. I know I'm small for eleven. But please, please don't call me baby.*

THIS IS WHAT A BABY LOOKS LIKE, MOM!

6
JUST A CHARACTER

"Honey," Mom said. "I wish you had a friend. I wish you had a nice kid to hang out with. Play your video games. You know? Connor Dunn's mom is in the church choir. Connor's in your class. You could be friends. He's a nice boy."

CONNOR DUNN
HAS COOL BRACES

Kemba said nothing. Connor was cool. He wasn't a bully. But Connor had lots of friends. He didn't need a loser like Kemba. If Mom asked Connor's mom? If she said anything? It would be like forcing Connor. Forcing him to hang with a kid he didn't like. Kemba didn't want that. Being alone was better. Who wanted to hang out because their moms made them?

"I don't like Connor," Kemba lied. So many lies.

Mom looked sad. "It hurts me to hear you sound so bitter."

Kemba got up. He grabbed his backpack. "Leave me alone, Mom." He headed for his room. Then he stopped. He looked back. His mom looked sad. Like she was going to cry.

"I'm sorry, Mom," Kemba said. "But I like being alone. Don't be mad."

"I'm not mad, honey," Mom said. "I'm just sorry."

"Don't be sorry. I'm happy. Okay?"

He went to his room. Did his math homework quickly. Then he got to what he really wanted. He turned on an Underdog game. It was a new one. Bright and exciting.

The game was about evil men. They used drones to scare people. The drones didn't look like planes. They looked like ghosts. Others looked like skeletons. They were remote controlled. They could fly low.

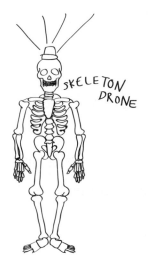

SKELETON DRONE

The drones' heads were red. They lit up. They swooped down. Attacked an old lady's house. She ran out screaming. Thought monsters were after her. But it was just a cruel joke.

OLD LADIES ARE NICE & GIVE YOU CANDY

Underdog brought the drones crashing down. Then he grabbed the two men who were playing the joke. "You don't pick on people," Underdog yelled. "Especially on poor old ladies." He gave both dudes a hard shake. Then he sent them running.

Underdog helped the old lady back to her house. He told her she was safe. "It was just a joke," he said.

Underdog was fierce in his costume. Especially with his eye patch. And he was a hero. Kemba loved him. He wasn't real. He was just a character. But to Kemba? He was his best friend.

UNDERDOG'S EYE PATCH FROM THE CAR CRASH

Kemba smiled to himself. Today had been pretty good. For a little while, Kemba was like Underdog. He scared off a mean kid. He helped Rozel. Rozel told him he was brave. It made Kemba feel like Underdog.

Mom and Dad loved him. But they wouldn't call him brave. They felt sorry for him. Today, he was strong. And brave. He took a risk. Maybe Jabar would have seen him. Maybe he would have come after him. Maybe he would have hurt him. Kemba had taken that risk. Now he grinned at his Underdog poster.

7
A BIGGER LOSER

Another day at school. Ms. Clay didn't say anything about what happened. Rozel probably didn't tell her. Kemba wasn't surprised. Why would Rozel tell her mom about Jabar? Kemba didn't tell his parents a lot of stuff either.

DERRICK NORRIS IS WORSE OFF THAN ME

Derrick Norris was worse off than Kemba. For sure Kemba was a loser. But

Derrick? He was way worse off. He was tall. Skinny. With bad acne. He wore thick glasses. He even stuttered sometimes. But only when he was nervous. Kemba thought Derrick was a sad case.

Kemba wanted to talk to Derrick. Or he thought he should. Maybe just say hello. But he was afraid to. He thought Derrick would stick to him. Kemba was unpopular enough. He did not need to team up. Not with a poor dude like Derrick.

Richie would laugh. He would make fun of them. A friendship between Kemba and Derrick? No way was that going to happen. That was why Kemba never even smiled at Derrick. He tried not to look at him. He felt guilty. But what could he do?

Nobody would look at Derrick. Not during lunch. Not during recess. Not in the halls. Kemba made sure not to look his way. He didn't want to give Derrick an opening.

But he was ashamed. Of himself. Of his classmates. Of his school. He didn't like himself very much. Underdog wouldn't do that.

At recess Kemba was near Connor. He was talking to one of his friends. Connor had lots of friends. "Yeah, there's gonna be drones all over. Man, it's so cool. It's the latest thing," he said.

"You mean those no-pilot planes?" the other kid asked.

"Yeah, dude," Connor said. "Some of them are big, like planes. But some are tiny. Some of them are no bigger than bugs." Connor laughed. He looked handsome when he laughed. Kemba wished he was like Connor. Good-looking. Popular. With lots of friends.

Kemba knew everybody envied Connor. He had it all. Kemba's mom thought they could be friends. That was too funny. No way. Connor and a nobody? Nuh-uh. He felt so small.

THIS IS HOW SMALL I FELT

"Some of the drones are like monsters," Connor said. "You know Sky Fear? I was playing it last night. Underdog let these bad dudes have it. They were using drones to scare an old lady. It was cool. Those dudes took off."

Kemba turned numb.

Connor played Underdog too? *Connor?* He didn't know why that surprised him.

"I like that superhero," Connor said. "Bringing those drones down? Scaring those bad guys? That was sweet."

"Yeah, he's cool," Connor's friend said. "I like Underdog too."

Kemba couldn't believe it.

Connor liked Underdog? And so did the

other kid.

Kemba wished he had the guts to go over. He could talk to Connor about Underdog. But he couldn't. It would sure make his mom happy. She wanted him to have a friend. She wanted him to talk to Connor. But that was crazy. Kemba froze at the thought. No way.

8
THE UNDERDOGS

It was the next day. Kids were getting to class. Connor came walking in with all his friends. They were smiling. Laughing. Cracking jokes.

Kemba smiled bitterly. Poor Mom. She lived in a dream world. Connor and Kemba? Uh-uh.

Then there was Derrick. Quiet. Alone.

Kemba thought he should at least say hi. That would be a kind thing. But he looked away when Derrick came in.

Richie came in. *Almost* late. Typical. He was not dumb enough to be late. Ms. Clay was tough. She wouldn't like it. Richie would get in trouble.

ALMOST LATE

Kemba was curious. Did Jabar tell his little brother what had happened? Probably not. Jabar would be ashamed to talk about it. He got scared. He ran. So he wouldn't want to admit that. Not to anybody.

Ms. Clay returned all the corrected

math homework. There was a big red A on Kemba's paper. Ms. Clay wrote, "The best work turned in. Way to go, Kemba!"

Kemba knew he should be proud. He should be happy. Mom would be proud. Dad would be proud.

But a great grade was not fun. Not if you couldn't share it. What good was it if you didn't have a friend? To talk to. To laugh with. To hang out with. Mom and Dad were great. But they weren't Kemba's friends. Only kids his age could be that.

Kemba felt a dull pain inside. He wanted a friend so bad. It hurt.

Underdog was alone. At first. He didn't have friends. Kemba remembered the first game. It was called "Underdog, the Beginning." As a kid, Underdog was teased. Other kids laughed at him. Pointed out how he looked. The missing eye. The patch. The scars from his accident. He was different. And kids were cruel.

A terrible car crash had injured Underdog. At first he was bitter. A loner. Then he decided he would spend his life helping others. He helped those who were ignored. Like he once was.

Underdog wore a black patch over his missing eye. His costume was black and purple. It had a yellow lightning bolt across the chest.

He looked great. He was handsome. The black patch made him look dangerous. Best of all? Everyone liked him. People cheered for him. He would shout, "I am Underdog!" He was a superhero. He did great things.

Because Underdog was mocked. And bullied. It made him the hero he was. He was kind to all. He had a big heart.

The bad guys in the games called him "one eye" or "pirate face." But he didn't turn bad. He didn't take his pain out on others. Instead, he helped the underdogs of the world. He became a friend to them. He would shout, "I am Underdog." Then the bullies would run. He was powerful. People loved him.

Kemba loved him more than anybody. Playing an Underdog game lifted Kemba up. Especially when he felt extra low.

9
FIVE WORDS

Kemba knew one thing for sure. Derrick was a sad case. He needed Underdog more than anybody at school. Kemba wished he had courage. Like Underdog. He would smile at Derrick. That would make the poor kid's day. Probably.

But he didn't say anything. Not to

Derrick. Not to anybody. He thought about it all during class. He even went over what he would say.

Hey, man. How's it going? So easy. So simple. *What's the big deal? I can say that. Right? I'll do it at lunch. Yeah!*

Just five little words.

He would do it. He would talk to Derrick.

SWEAT

As lunch neared, Kemba got nervous. It was getting closer. Time was running out. He would say something to Derrick. Kemba pictured Richie seeing it happen. He'd laugh his head off. Then his friends would join in. When Richie laughed, all his friends joined in. It was a signal. Richie did something. His friends did it too.

Kemba and Derrick would be standing there. All the bullies would be around them. Laughing. Teasing them.

Kemba got more nervous.

He couldn't do it. Not today. Maybe tomorrow. Yeah, maybe tomorrow. He just wasn't brave enough to do it today. Kemba kept seeing what would happen. He and Derrick would be a pair. A pair of fools. A pair of losers. And Richie would beat them down.

A PAIR OF LOSERS

Kemba felt small. Gutless. He headed for lunch. Down the halls. Eyes low. Watching for Derrick. Derrick usually got his lunch last. He didn't want any trouble.

Kemba walked behind Connor and one of his friends. They were talking about last night's big game. They were laughing about the quarterback. About all the fumbles.

"That number eighteen! He was losing the ball on every play. What a dud. He must have had butter on his fingers. He ruined it for the Panthers in front of the home fans," Connor's friend said.

"Yeah. He was having a bad night," Connor said. "But I felt sorry for the guy. I've seen him play great. Even the pros have bad games. Look at the last Super Bowl. One of the best quarterbacks of all time. His team down by forty points or something."

Kemba wondered at that. Why Connor would have sympathy for a rich baller? That dude was lucky. Playing pro ball. Making millions. Connor didn't even give Derrick a wave. Couldn't he see Derrick was a sad case? What was up? Why was that?

MY FAVORITE LUNCH!

Kemba got a look at lunch. He was glad. Usually the school's lunches were awful. Wilted salad greens. Flimsy pink tomatoes with no taste. Rubbery cheese. Sawdust chicken nuggets. Soggy fries. But today looked good. Really good!

There was sweet and sour chicken. Fluffy

rice. Kemba's mom made great sweet and sour chicken. He loved it. It was his favorite dish. This looked almost as good. Pineapple chunks and carrot slices in the salad too. And for dessert? Sweet potato pie. Kemba grinned.

10
THE STAND

Derrick was right behind Kemba. He seemed happy about lunch too. His eyes widened. Kemba noticed them behind Derrick's thick glasses.

Then Kemba said, "Looks good for a change, huh?"

"Yeah!" Derrick said. He almost smiled.

That was it. The first time. Ever. That

Kemba had said a word to Derrick. Let alone six.

Kemba loaded up his tray. Started for the lunch tables.

And then it happened.

Richie and another kid smashed into Derrick. His tray went flying. The sweet and sour chicken landed on the dirty floor. The sauce mingled with the dust. All the fluffy rice scattered. The salad was crushed under Richie's big feet. The pineapple chunks were mashed. The carrot slices had shoe marks.

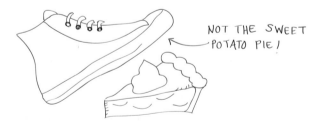

NOT THE SWEET POTATO PIE!

Then they smashed the sweet potato pie.

Derrick's lunch was ruined.

Kemba heard a strange cry. Like the moaning of a hurt animal. It wasn't loud. It was almost like something … dying.

"Sorry, dude," Richie said. "Lost my balance. Tripped." He started laughing. He and his buddy were laughing hard. They almost choked.

Kemba stared at Derrick. The tall boy with bad acne and thick glasses. The boy who stuttered. The sad loser. The boy no one talked to. He was going to have one good thing today. A nice lunch. Just one good thing. Now it was gone.

Something flowed through Kemba. He didn't know what was happening. He was hot. Shaking with a rage he'd never felt. His face was boiling. His eyes were bulging. His fingers clenched into fists. He was going to lose it.

"You're evil, Richie Mason! You stinking creep!" Kemba screamed. "You buy Derrick another lunch. Or else!"

ME, OUT-OF THIS-WORLD ANGRY

Richie and his friend snorted. But then another boy stepped forward. Stood next to Kemba.

"I'm with Kem, man," Connor Dunn shouted. "You clean up that mess. Dude, that was low. Get Derrick another lunch!"

Then there were others. Boys and girls.

"Do what Kem says."

"Now, dude."

"Shake a leg!"

"Jerk!"

"Clean it up!"

The faces of the kids flamed with anger.

Richie and his friend stopped laughing. They cleaned up the ruined lunch. Then they got a new lunch for Derrick. Richie even said he was sorry. Though he wasn't. Not really.

Everyone came up to Derrick. They made sure he was okay. Even Kemba.

Then Kemba sat down to eat. Connor came to Kemba's lunch table. "Mind if I join you?" he asked.

"Uh, no," Kemba said. "Sure. Sit." He still hadn't gotten over the nickname—Kem. He never had a nickname before. It was a big deal.

"Kem," Connor said. "I hated what Richie did to Derrick. But I don't think I woulda jumped on it. Not like you did. That was cool, man."

Kemba didn't know what to say. He grinned.

"You know who you remind me of, dude?" Connor said. "My favorite superhero. From my favorite game. Underdog."

"That's my favorite game too," Kemba said. "Thanks."

Kemba had thought the sweet and sour chicken was the best thing to happen that day. But he thought wrong. He spoke up. He yelled at a bully. He defended Derrick. And Connor talked to him. Ate lunch at his table. Bringing all his friends with him.

"See you tomorrow, Underdog," Connor said after lunch. The boys high-fived.